A Sound Like Someone Trying Not to Make a Sound

A story by John Irving

Illustrated by Tatjana Hauptmann

A Doubleday Book for Young Readers

A Sound Like Someone Trying Not to Make a Sound is a children's story
found within John Irving's novel *A Widow for One Year.*
This story has now been illustrated by Tatjana Hauptmann.

A Doubleday Book for Young Readers

Published by
Random House Children's Books
a division of
Random House, Inc.
New York

Doubleday and the anchor with dolphin colophon are registered trademarks of
Random House, Inc.

Visit us on the Web! www.randomhouse.com/kids
Educators and librarians, for a variety of teaching tools, visit us at
www.randomhouse.com/teachers

Library of Congress Cataloging-in-Publication Data is available upon request.

ISBN: 0-385-74680-6 (trade)
0-385-90910-1 (lib. bdg.)

The text of this book is set in 16.5-point Bembo.
MANUFACTURED IN THE U.S.A.
September 2004
10 9 8 7 6 5 4 3 2

INTRODUCTION

In my ninth novel, *A Widow for One Year,* I created a character named Ted Cole, a most *un*sympathetic writer of stories for children. Years of reading children's books to my own three sons has given me a low opinion of the kind of children's literature that is intent on frightening the very young; there is a long, stubborn tradition of it. In creating Ted Cole (one of the more willful villains in my novels), I was conscious of taking such an author to task.

The darkest of Ted Cole's stories for children is called "The Door in the Floor." (A good title, a creepy story.) But "A Sound Like Someone Trying Not to Make a Sound" is somewhat different. It is the gentlest of Ted Cole's stories—the title (the phrase itself) is something Ted hears his five-year-old daughter, Ruth, say. And because Ted Cole tells it to Ruth to help her forget a nightmare, it has a sweeter motive than do the stories Ted usually writes.

I am grateful to Winfried Stephan at Diogenes Verlag, my German-language publisher, for the idea to publish "A Sound Like Someone Trying Not to Make a Sound" in book form; and also to Diogenes for persuading their marvelous illustrator, the artist Tatjana Hauptmann, to bring this story to such rich visual life.

I am not a children's book author. But in creating this story, I was conscious of the many times I tried to comfort my children, to coax them back to sleep after they'd suffered one nightmare or another. This is the story that, to me, made the most sense of nightmares. I gave it as a gift to my character Ted Cole—just as Ted's daughter, Ruth, gives him the title for the story.

Tom woke up, but Tim did not. It was the middle of the night.

"Did you hear that?"
Tom asked his brother.

But Tim was only two.
Even when he was awake, he didn't talk much.

Tom woke up his
father and asked him:
"Did you hear
that sound?"

"What did it sound like?" his father asked.

"It sounded like a monster with no arms and no legs, but it was trying to move," Tom said.

"How could it move with no arms and no legs?" his father asked.

"It wriggles," Tom said. "It slides on its fur."

"Oh, it has fur?" his father asked.

"It pulls itself along with its teeth," Tom said.

"It has teeth, too!" his father exclaimed.

"I told you—it's a monster!" Tom said.

"But what exactly was the sound that woke you up?" his father asked.

"It was a sound like, in the closet, if one of Mommy's dresses came alive and it tried to climb down off the hanger," Tom said.

"Let's go back to your room and listen for the sound," Tom's father said.

And there was Tim, still asleep—he still hadn't heard the sound.

It was a sound like someone pulling the nails out of the floorboards under the bed. It was a sound like a dog trying to open a door. Its mouth was wet, so it couldn't get a good grip on the doorknob, but it wouldn't stop trying—eventually the dog would get in, Tom thought.

It was a sound like a ghost in the attic, dropping the peanuts it had stolen from the kitchen.

It was a sound like someone trying not to make a sound.

"There's the sound again!" Tom whispered to his father. "Did you hear that?"

This time, Tim woke up, too. It was a sound like something caught inside the headboard of the bed. It was eating its way out—it was gnawing through the wood.

It seemed to Tom that the sound was definitely the sound of an armless, legless monster dragging its thick, wet fur.

"It's a monster!" Tom cried.

"It's just a mouse crawling between the walls,"
his father said.

Tim screamed. He didn't know what a "mouse" was.
It frightened him to think of something with wet, thick
fur—and no arms and no legs—crawling between the walls.
How did something like that get between the walls,
anyway?

But Tom asked his father, "It's just a mouse?"

His father thumped against the wall with his hand
and they listened to the mouse scurrying away. "If it comes
back again," he said to Tom and Tim, "just hit the wall."

"A mouse crawling between the walls!" said Tom.
"That's all it was!"

He quickly fell asleep, and his father went back to bed and fell asleep, too, but Tim was awake the whole night long, because he didn't know what a mouse was and he wanted to be awake when the thing crawling between the walls came crawling back.

Each time he thought he heard the mouse crawling between the walls, Tim hit the wall with his hand and the mouse scurried away—dragging its thick, wet fur and its no arms and legs with it.

And that is the end of the story.